Little FRIENDS

by **Onur Tukel**

Marshall Cavendish Children

Dedicated to my awesome mom and dad
and special thanks to Margery Cuyler, Anahid Hamparian,
David Thayer French, and Daniel Kraus

Text and illustrations copyright © 2012 by Onur Tukel
All rights reserved
Marshall Cavendish Corporation, 99 White Plains Road, Tarrytown, NY 10591
www.marshallcavendish.us/kids

Library of Congress Cataloging-in-Publication Data
Tukel, Onur.
Little friends / written and illustrated by Onur Tukel. —1st ed.
p. cm.
Summary: Best friends Sara and Louisa are drawn into a friendship with
their neighbor Barry, who rarely speaks with anyone, as they all enjoy
playing near the huge old tree at the top of the hill.
ISBN 978-0-7614-6260-6 (hardcover) — ISBN 978-0-7614-6261-3 (ebook)
[1. Best friends—Fiction. 2. Friendship—Fiction. 3. Trees—Fiction.] I.
Title.
PZ7.T8229635Lit 2012
[E]—dc23
2011029522

The illustrations are rendered in pencil and ink, scanned, and colored digitally.
Book design by Anahid Hamparian
Editor: Margery Cuyler

Printed in Malaysia (T)
First edition
1 3 5 6 4 2

Marshall Cavendish
Children

Contents

Chapter 1
The Tire Swing

Sara and Louisa
were neighbors.

They did everything together.

They studied together.

They danced together.

They laughed together.

They were best friends.

5

A little boy lived across the street.

His name was Barry.

Barry rarely talked to anyone.

One afternoon, while playing in their neighborhood, Louisa and Sara noticed something strange.

Someone was swinging from a tire on the tree at the top of the hill.

"Isn't that Barry?" Louisa asked.

"I think it is," Sara answered.

They watched Barry swing back and forth.

"That looks like fun," said Louisa.

The next day, Louisa and Sara
climbed the hill.

"Let's swing,"
Louisa said.

"This is fun!"
Sara laughed.

When Barry
arrived, he
got mad.

"Why are you riding *my* tire swing?" he asked.

"Because it's fun," Louisa said.

"But I didn't give you permission," Barry yelled.

"We don't need your permission," said Louisa.

Barry stormed off.

The next day, Sara and Louisa found a sign nailed to the tree.

When Barry arrived, Sara asked him, "So . . . may we ride on your tire swing now?"

"No," Barry said. "You may not!"

"Don't you know it's nice to share things?" Louisa said.

"I don't care!" Barry barked back.

"Fine!" Louisa said, and the girls left in a huff.

13

The next afternoon, Louisa and Sara found a tire of their own and rolled it up the hill.

They hung it from a branch on the opposite side of the tree.

When Barry showed up, he was furious.

"I didn't give you permission
to hang a tire swing on the
other side of this tree!"
he yelled.

"We don't need your permission!"
Louisa cried.

Barry stormed off.

That night, Barry returned to the tree with his parents' hedge clippers.

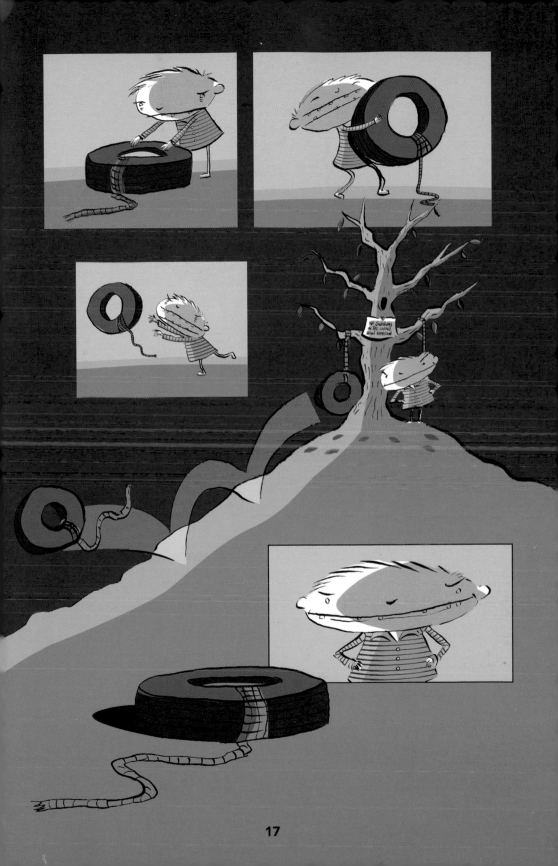

Louisa and Sara were shocked when they saw the broken rope.

"Who would do such a thing?"
Sara asked.

NO SWINGING
ON TIRE SWING
WITHOUT PERMISSION

"I know who,"
Louisa said.

Louisa returned the next day with her own pair of hedge clippers.

NO SWINGING ON TIRE SWING WITHOUT PERMISSION

"Don't do this," Sara said. "It's mean."

"He deserves it," Louisa said.

Louisa cut through half the rope.
Just then, Sara spotted Barry
walking up the hill.

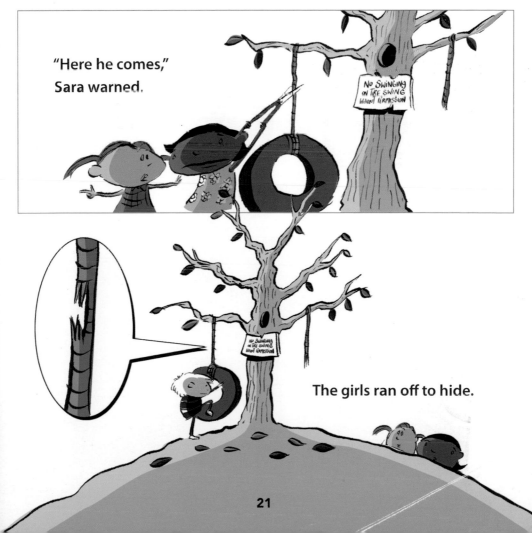

"Here he comes,"
Sara warned.

The girls ran off to hide.

21

What happened next was not good.

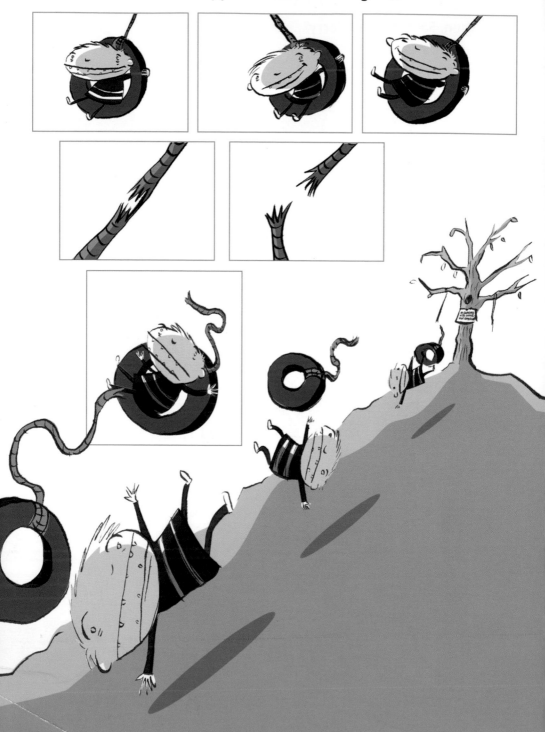

"Oh no!" cried Louisa.

The girls rushed
down the hill.

"Are you okay?" Sara asked.

"I think so," Barry said. He was
a bit dazed. "What happened?"

"We cut the rope on your tire swing," Sara explained.

"That's not true," Louisa exclaimed. "*I* cut the rope. Sara thought it was a bad idea."

"Aren't you going to apologize?" Barry asked.

"Apologize?" Louisa shouted. "Why should we? You cut down our tire swing first."

"Well, you almost got me killed!" Barry yelled.

"Don't be so dramatic!" Louisa cried.
"You just took a little tumble!"

Barry looked up at the tree. Maybe Louisa was right. He hadn't really gotten hurt. And none of this would have happened if he hadn't acted first.

"Let's drop the whole thing," said Sara.

"Come on, Louisa, let's go home."

Barry was alone. Again.

The next day, Sara and Louisa walked their dogs by Barry's house.

"Should we ask him to come outside?" Sara asked.

"I guess," Louisa said.

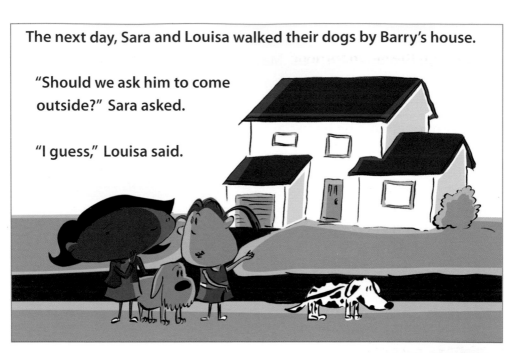

The girls rang Barry's doorbell.
"Wanna help us walk our dogs?" they asked.

"Okay," said Barry.

Louisa, Barry, and Sara spent the day walking their dogs through the neighborhood.

Together . . .

. . . as friends.

Chapter 2
The Snow Fortress

When it snowed, Louisa and Sara put on their winter clothes and raced outside to build a snowman.

"Let's see if Barry wants to come out and play," Sara said.

They knocked on Barry's door, but no one answered.

"I guess he's not home," Louisa said.

Later that day, Louisa and Sara decided to go sledding. When they walked to the field, they saw a large snow fort up on the hill.

"I wonder who built that?" Louisa asked.

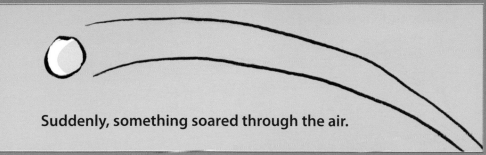

Suddenly, something soared through the air.

PLOP!

"Hey!"

"Who threw that?"

Then came another snowball,

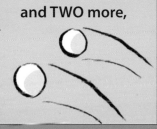

and TWO more,

and FOUR more!

"They're coming from the fortress!" cried Sara.

Louisa and Sara moved back a safe distance.

"Who's up there?"
Louisa called.

A head popped up from behind
the fortress wall.

It was Barry.

"I am king of the hilltop," he announced. "I have built a fortress to protect this mighty tree of power which controls the universe. If you can break down these walls, *you* will control the universe!"

"What's he talking about?" Louisa asked.
"I have no idea," Sara said.

"It's just a game!"
Barry called.

"See if you can climb the hill and enter the fortress!"

"I get it," Louisa said. "If we can enter the fortress, we win the game."

"That sounds easy," Sara said.

"Come on!"

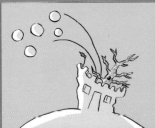

"Okay!"

"Let's go for it!!!"

Louisa and Sara tried to climb the hill.

But Barry kept bombarding them with snowballs.

They had no choice but to run away.

"I've got an idea," Louisa said. "You circle around the other side of the hill, and I'll run up this side.

He can't hit us both if we're on opposite sides."

But Sara and Louisa were wrong.

They didn't conquer the fortress.

The fortress conquered them.

"Better luck tomorrow!"
Barry yelled.

The two girls walked home.

"How does he do it?"
Sara asked. "His
snowballs are so
fast."

"And accurate," Louisa added.

"If we're going to conquer the fortress, we have to come up with a secret plan," Sara said.

Louisa looked at the snowman they had built earlier.

She pressed some snow into a snowball.

She took aim,

and she threw it.

It hit the snowman right on his carrot nose.

"Hey," Louisa said. "I've got a great idea!"

The next morning, Barry got up bright and early and headed for the fortress.

When he got to the field, he was shocked to see . . .

. . . dozens and dozens of snowmen.

They were everywhere!

Then Barry saw Louisa and Sara.

He ran up to the fortress.

"Are you ready to play?" the girls called.

"Ready when you are!"

Louisa ran left. Sara ran right. They each ducked behind a snowman!

Barry flung snowball after snowball.

None of them hit the girls.

They hit the snowmen instead.

The girls quickly weaved their way around the snowmen and up the hill until finally . . .

. . . they conquered the fortress.

"I guess I'm not the king of the hilltop anymore," said Barry.

"Now we can all be kings and control the universe," Sara said.

"Yeah!" exclaimed Louisa.

"I don't think this game is fun anymore," Barry said.

"Let's go sledding."

Chapter 3
The Tree Stump

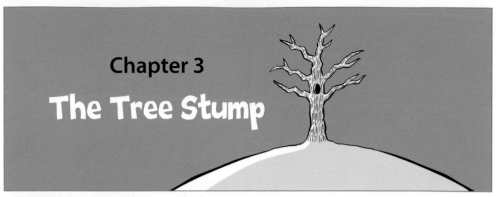

It was spring and the weather was getting warmer.

Sara, Barry, and Louisa spent their afternoons playing outside.

They even hung a new tire swing.

One day, it started to rain and they had to run home.

They played cards at Barry's house while the storm pounded the roof.

They could see the storm raging through the window.

They could hear the wind howling outside.

The storm raged for hours. Suddenly, the children heard a loud . . .

"Our special tree!" cried Sara.

The next day, Barry, Sara, and Louisa watched a lumberjack cut up the tree and load the pieces onto a truck.

"What will you do with all that wood?" Louisa asked.

"It will be used for lots of things," the lumberjack said.

"Some of the pieces might be used to build a house. An artist might use a piece to make a wood sculpture. A furniture maker could use it to make a bureau."

"Don't worry. None of this wood will go to waste," he added. Then he drove away.

The three friends stared at where the tree had stood so tall the night before. All that remained was a flat, wooden stump.

"I wish we could make our tree come back," Sara said.

"Well," Louisa said, "if the tree is going to be recycled, maybe its stump could be used for something else."

"I doubt it," Barry said. "A stump just isn't the same as a tree."

"I think Louisa is right," Sara said. "Let's come up with ways to use the tree stump. We can share our ideas tomorrow after school."

"Okay," said Louisa.

"I won't have any ideas," said Barry.

"You won't know unless you try," said Sara.

After dinner that night, Barry wanted to play with his hand puppet.

But he couldn't find it anywhere.

Louisa helped her father bake cookies. They tasted bland.

Sara painted a picture but wasn't sure how to finish it.

They were all too busy to think about the tree stump.

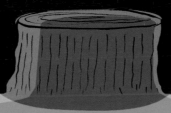

The next day, Sara, Barry, and Louisa met on the hill.

"I give up," Barry said. "There's nothing we can do with an old tree stump."

"I agree," said Louisa.

But Sara wasn't sure.

"There must be a way to use this stump," Sara thought.
"I'll think of something, even if I have to sit here the rest
of the day!"

Until something incredible happened.

A river of ideas began to flow into Sara's head.

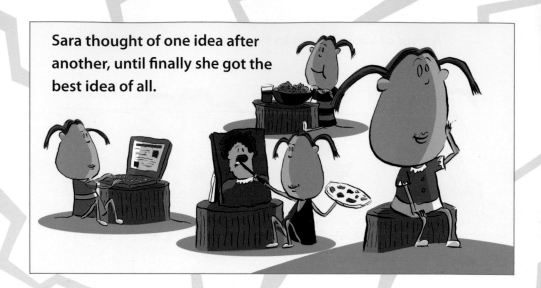

Sara thought of one idea after another, until finally she got the best idea of all.

"This stump should be used for thinking!"

"I have to tell Louisa and Barry!"

"You're out of your mind," Barry said.

"I'm not out of my mind," Sara said. "I'm *inside* my mind. That's the point!"

"Follow me!"

"Now sit down and see what happens!"

Barry thought about where he had left his hand puppet. "Bruno must have buried it in the backyard!"

Louisa thought about the cookies that she'd baked with her father. "Maybe they'd taste better with raisins and chocolate chips."

Sara thought about her painting. Then an idea hit her. "I'll paint a hot-air balloon in the corner!"

The three friends rejoiced. **Thinking was fun!**

All spring and summer, the children went to the stump to think. Sometimes they brought books to read, because you have to think when you read. Sometimes they wrote down their thoughts. Sometimes they played games.

Each day, they felt a little smarter than they had the day before.

When the sun started to set, the three friends went home. But they always returned to their tree stump, because . . .

. . . there was always something to think about!